TRUE BLUE

TRUE BLUE

Sigmund Brouwer
& Cindy Morgan

ORCA BOOK PUBLISHERS

Library and Archives Canada Cataloguing in Publication

Brouwer, Sigmund, 1959–, author
True blue / Sigmund Brouwer, Cindy Morgan.
(Orca limelights)

Issued in print and electronic formats.
ISBN 978-1-4598-1580-3 (softcover).—ISBN 978-1-4598-1581-0 (pdf).—
ISBN 978-1-4598-1582-7 (epub)

I. Morgan, Cindy, 1968–, author II. Title. III. Series: Orca limelights
PS8553.R68467T78 2018   jc813'.54   C2017-904484-2
C2017-904485-0

First published in the United States, 2018
Library of Congress Control Number: 2017949717

Summary: Elle has everything she's ever dreamed of,
but can she hold on to it?

*Orca Book wPublishers is dedicated to preserving the environment and has printed
this book on Forest Stewardship Council® certified paper.*

Orca Book Publishers gratefully acknowledges the support for
its publishing programs provided by the following agencies:
the Government of Canada through the Canada Book Fund and the Canada
Council for the Arts, and the Province of British Columbia through the
BC Arts Council and the Book Publishing Tax Credit.

Cover photography by iStock.com/sdominick
Edited by Tanya Trafford

ORCA BOOK PUBLISHERS
www.orcabook.com

Printed and bound in Canada.

21 20 19 18 • 4 3 2 1

To Olivia and Savannah.
You fill our lives with beautiful colors.

One

All the muscles in Elle's throat started to constrict as she tried not to panic.

Everything had been going so well until now.

The crowd was on fire, clapping to the beat of her song. The lights were moving in time with the music. She felt beautiful in her glittery blue dress and brown vintage cowboy boots. Her headset allowed her to move around the stage. Her jewel-studded guitar strap held her guitar close enough to her to make it easy for her to play, sing and move freely.

She was flying high.

Until her voice cracked at the climax of the high note. Blaine, the bass player, caught her eye and raised his eyebrows. She struggled through the last three songs in her set, trying not to think too much about her voice. But hearing her voice crack over a gigantic sound system in a huge arena was one of the most embarrassing and terrifying things she had ever experienced.

The band gave her high fives at the end. She held her hand up to her throat, and Blaine said, "Don't worry, Elle. It happens to everyone. Even Johnny's voice cracks once in a while. It's part of singing live."

"Yeah, but he's Johnny James," Elle said. "With twenty thousand screaming fans every night, I don't know if they even hear him singing."

Blaine tilted his head. "I know what you mean, but still...don't worry about it. Get a little extra rest. There's some Throat Coat tea in the green room. Just go straight to bed on the bus tonight. I bet you wake up good as new."

She appreciated him being straight with her. Elle had never been on any tour before, much less the biggest sold-out tour in country music. It was all part of a life she was just beginning to understand.

Johnny's twin backup singers ignored her as she passed them backstage. They were probably thrilled her voice had cracked. Many backup singers, Elle knew, were waiting for their big break. Wondering why they weren't the ones out in front.

* * *

Elle understood how you could end up with a bad attitude in this business. When she'd first come to Nashville, she'd been overconfident. All her friends and family had told her how talented she was. How she was going make it big fast.

It hadn't happened.

She remembered the first time she'd gone to the Bluebird Cafe. It was a world-famous hole-in-the-wall-dive where the world's most esteemed songwriters came to play the big hits they'd written for other artists. There was so much talent. That's when she had discovered that the bar was set very high in Nashville. You didn't get close to reaching that bar without some tough life lessons, which often turned into songs.

She had been knocked down and gotten back up more times than she cared to remember. But those hard knocks had taught her a little something about humility. About learning from others and not acting like a know-it-all brat. She had songwriter friends to thank for teaching her that. But she wasn't a pushover. Humility doesn't mean you can't have confidence. Elle was learning to trust her instincts.

Elle made her way to the green room. The Throat Coat tea was on the catering table along with hot water, lemon and honey. A huge fruit platter sat in the center of the table with fancy granola bars, hummus and pita chips on either side. There was even a little espresso machine for those who needed a serious boost before going onstage. The crew guys went for the monster drinks and Gatorade. The singers pampered themselves with designer water. Only the best for Johnny James and his band and crew.

Elle filled her travel mug with hot water, a tea bag and some honey. When she took a sip, it felt good sliding down her raspy throat.

Yes, life in the big leagues was everything she'd imagined. But the day in, day out grind of touring wasn't as easy as she had thought it would be.

A lot had happened since she had posted a YouTube video that revealed how she had been transformed by her record company from Charlene into Elle. The dieting, the skanky clothes, the makeover. How it had made her feel a lot less than authentic. How she was taking that back.

And then her big break had arrived.

She still remembered the phone call from her father, telling her the amazing news.

Guess what artist wants you to open for him? he'd asked.

Not in a million years would she have guessed that Johnny James wanted her on his tour.

At first, it had seemed like a dream. All those years writing and singing songs in her bedroom had brought her to Nashville. Her first days there had been rough. Her first producer had turned out to be a complete crook. Thankfully, one wonderful thing had come out of that awful time. She had met Webb, who had been swindled by the same producer.

His full name was Jim Webb, but most people just called him Webb. When Elle's (and Webb's) label had gone under, Webb had been a rock for Elle. When her father bought the label, Webb had reminded her that she didn't have to be anything but true to herself.

Since then, Webb had chosen the indie route and was building quite a following through social media. His YouTube channel was actually earning him money every day.

Elle also had a YouTube channel that was doing well, but there was no doubt that being on a major label created many more opportunities for an artist. Now, living life out on the road, Elle was just beginning to understand the not-so-glamorous part about being a touring artist.

The tour had started off better than anything she had dreamed of. Big tours tended to start off in cities on the smaller, midwestern circuit. Places where people weren't music critics in the same way they were in entertainment towns like Nashville, LA, Atlanta and New York.

She remembered how nervous she had been when she first stepped in front of a sold-out crowd in Minneapolis, in her home state. Twenty thousand screaming fans in an arena bigger than anything she'd ever seen in her small town.

The scariest part wasn't the singing. For her it was the talking. She had gone through months of public-relations coaching with a woman named Karen in Nashville. Karen was legendary in the music business for getting young, not-so-well-spoken newbies ready to do interviews.

Elle remembered her first session with Karen, who had videotaped Elle answering a series of questions. When they were done, Karen had played the video back for Elle.

Elle, what do you hope your music accomplishes in the world? Karen had asked.

Um, well, like, I hope that, um, like, my music will connect.

Elle had wanted to crawl under her chair. She had no idea she spoke that way.

Look, Elle, Karen said, *the way you speak is very typical for teens. But you are not just a typical "teen" anymore. You are a national recording artist for Starstruck Records. The expectation is that you will be well spoken.*

Like Taylor Swift? Elle asked. She had been impressed when she saw Taylor Swift on *Good*

Morning America. She had been so poised and confident.

Yes, Taylor is a very bright and poised young woman. Now. When she first came to me, she sounded just like you, Karen said.

You worked with Taylor? For some reason, Elle was totally amazed.

Yes. But again, she wasn't a pro when she first sat in that chair. But with enough time and practice, you will be just as poised as Taylor.

Elle nodded. After all, if Taylor could do it, why couldn't she?

After that first show in Minneapolis, Elle had given her first series of interviews for tour press. She had taken deep breaths, remembering what Karen had taught her. *Think of the first word you are going to say before you form the first sentence. Don't stall with an um or like.* It was very effective, and though Elle wasn't Taylor yet, she was getting there.

Two

lle made her way back to her dressing room to change into her sweats and pack up for the bus. Most nights she went to the product table to meet new fans and sign what she sold. Her new EP was her big seller. A close second was a huge poster from her last photo shoot. She also carried a vintage-style T-shirt that was big with her female fans. Younger fans liked autographed head shots.

Tonight, she had told their tour manager, Todd, that she was going to skip the product table. She hated to let her fans down, but she didn't want to risk straining her voice further by talking a lot right after a show.

She stuffed her cowboy boots into the boot drawer of the stage wardrobe that was brought into her dressing room every night. Her clothes would appear in the wardrobe before the next show, clean, steamed and ready to wear. She'd been pretty excited about it the first day of rehearsal. Now it was just part of her routine.

That first day, her head had spun when a rack of beautiful designer clothing was presented to her. Her stylist, Kara Kat, pulled out a lot of skimpy options.

Do you have anything with a bit more, um, fabric? Elle asked. *You know how I feel about this kind of stuff.*

Kara rolled her eyes. *We've been over this before, Elle! It's all about your image. And these are the images approved by your label's marketing department.* Her sidekick, Brian, stood behind her, nodding his head in agreement.

That all changed when Elle called her dad that night.

He sent an email to the stylist, requesting that Elle's clothing choices be respected.

He was the boss, so Kara begrudgingly obliged. Mel and Shel, the twin background singers, were more than happy to wear the skimpy outfits Elle had rejected.

There had been many discussions about Elle's "look," but in the end, she decided she liked the idea of wearing dresses—a little on the short side but not too short—and boots. Something feminine and a little glam, with the boots to keep it earthy.

Kara and Brian faked enthusiasm for her wardrobe choices, obviously sucking back their resentment at having their creativity questioned by a newbie.

Elle felt it all, but she tried to remember what her mother had taught her and what had become her core belief in life—be true to yourself. Even if other people don't like it.

Elle tried not to take advantage of her relationship with the label owner too often, but he was her dad. And he probably didn't really want her prancing around onstage in next to nothing anyway.

About halfway through the first rehearsal, Elle had been brought to the side of the stage to meet Johnny James. He was even better-looking in person than he was in his videos. Elle had thought she would faint when he said, *I love that song of yours "True Blue." Sounds awesome.*

Your voice is killer, not to mention you're pretty easy on the eyes.

He had topped this off with a smile so charming that, as they said in the south, it could have melted butter. *Looking forward to having you out on the tour, sweetheart,* he said.

He gave her a hug, and she was swept back to the stage for rehearsal.

The band sounded like a recording. Johnny James could afford to hire the very best and hottest players in Nashville. But it wasn't only about skill. It was also about having stage presence and fitting a certain persona. Elle wasn't too thrilled to see Jack Miles, an arrogant guitar player she'd met when her friend Marsha used him on a session. It hadn't gone well.

Blaine, the bass player, seemed nice. Will, on drums, was the funny guy. Scott on keys was a brilliant computer geek who kept to himself. But when they came together to make music, it was mind-blowing.

She'd left the rehearsal feeling giddy and euphoric, hardly able to believe that she was going to be singing on a huge stage in front of thousands of people.

Back then, she couldn't wait for the tour to begin.

Now, she was worried that it would be over for her all too soon.

Three

Go ahead, tell me how awesome you were! The text was from Webb. She smiled. He always knew what to say to make her feel better.

She texted back. **Hmm...not so awesome tonight, but it will be ok. You ok? How's life on the houseboat?**

Elle visited Webb on his houseboat whenever she was home in Nashville. She liked to gaze through the skylight at the stars as they listened to the water lapping against the dock.

Webb said it was the best piece of real estate in Nashville. He was housesitting for the friend of a friend. His family was in Canada. The music was in Nashville.

He sent an emoji with stars in its eyes. **Nashville isn't the same without you.**

She sent back one with blushing cheeks.
I gotta go watch Johnny's show.

Ok. Lata.

*   *   *

Elle took another long drink from her mug as she walked to the sprawling black tour bus to put her bag in the luggage bay. There was still a little down time before Johnny's show began. She liked to watch it from the wings of the stage, next to Simon at the monitor board.

Simon was the sound guy who ran the "inner ears"—the custom-made earbuds each musician wore to hear the sound mix. He always had a stool beside him at the board, so she could have a clear view of everything happening onstage.

Simon and all the other sound and crew guys worked hard every day, setting up the stage each morning and then breaking it down each night. They were up early while everyone else was sleeping in.

Elle liked Simon. He had a small athletic frame. She'd seen him scramble up the lighting rigs, and you had to be pretty fit to climb up in the rafters. He was quiet but gave off an air of confidence. He always had a kind word for Elle. She sat and drank her tea in comfortable silence while Simon turned knobs and tested everyone's earbud levels.

There were no cables or monitors to trip over when Johnny James was running all over the stage, doing a choreographed dance number with groups of local dancers. It was quite a production.

Simon signaled the band and spoke into their monitors. "Showtime, boys—everybody ready?" The lights dimmed to black. There was always a lot of suspense as the crew operated the rigging that would raise Johnny on a flying platform high above the crowd.

The lights began to swirl, the music grew in intensity, and then Johnny made his big entrance. The crowd went insane. The girls lined up for rows and rows at the front screamed and cried out his name. It was a little out of control, but the sense of drama was exciting. Even after having seen it six times now, it still gave Elle chills.

Drama.

Performing was about creating drama. And there was no lack of drama on the road.

At intermission, Johnny walked offstage on her side. Elle gave him a big thumbs-up. He winked at her and gave her a brief shoulder rub. Elle felt her stomach do a flip. Nope—life on the road wasn't all bad. She just had to get some sleep tonight. She could feel an ache in her throat. No staying up late on the bus or else her voice would be toast.

Four

Elle would never forget her first run-in with the twins. It had happened on the bus.

Now, does everyone know the bus rules? Todd had said.

Everyone nodded and smiled except Elle. She had no idea what the bus rules were, so she raised her hand. Todd looked down at her and smiled.

Okay, these are bus rules. No putting toilet paper in the toilet. Put your TP in the trash can. And no number twos! If you're desperate, go to the driver, and he'll find a truck stop. So no TP down the tube and no number twos!

Elle was beyond embarrassed. One of the band guys patted her on the back and said, *Don't worry, Elle. Someone had to tell us about the bus rules when we were newbies.*

She smiled and shrank in her little seat behind the booth that served as an eating area.

At least the twins hadn't witnessed her being told the bus rules, but she wondered when they would be arriving. She'd asked Blaine about it, and he'd told her that the twins rode on Johnny's bus. She'd felt a little strange being the only girl on the band bus. When she told her dad about it, he called Todd, who put the two background singers back on the band bus.

It was obvious almost immediately that they were less than thrilled at being taken off Johnny's bus. They'd sauntered onto the bus in short bright-orange terry-cloth shorts with the word *bootylicious* stitched across their backsides.

They each carried a Louis Vuitton designer duffel bag in one hand and a large stuffie to sleep with in the other. They were a strange mix of vixen and Barbie doll.

When Blaine asked why they were on the band bus, Shelly said, *Oh, someone went running to Daddy, and here we are.* Mel had stood beside Shel, her hand on her hip and her eyes narrowing on Elle.

Elle had felt her face go bright red.

Rumor was, Shel had a massive crush on Johnny, who was newly married to a young LA actress named Holly Haddison. Elle was sure he had no interest in Shel.

*   *   *

The next day when Elle was at the hotel getting ready for soundcheck, she got a FaceTime call from Webb. She could tell that he was in a studio.

He'd been picking up work playing on a few hot indie records. Every few years Nashville had a new "it" guy. A player that all the tastemakers in town got excited about. One of the up-and-coming artists who played in small clubs and cafés to small but appreciative crowds. People who were aware of small nuances and subtle genius. Stuff that was lost on those who only went in for big mainstream artists.

Webb seemed to be well on his way to being the new "it" guy. His latest EP was a collection of poetic songs set to moody melodies with a hook. They matched his clean, emotional guitar skills.

Lots of people had heard about him being ripped off by a shady producer when he first came to town. They knew he lived on a houseboat and busked for a living and had been discovered by Nashville legend Harley Hays.

It was the kind of stuff that Nashville dreams were built on.

"Yeah, I was thinking about you, wondering how the tour was going," Webb said. "They don't need me for a minute, so I thought I'd check in."

Elle loved hearing about his day, getting a peek inside his world. It seemed so much less stressful than her life on the road.

"So hey. How goes it on the road?" he asked.

"It's going," Elle replied.

"It must be pretty amazing. I read some of the reviews. The critics say the opener is rocking the stage every night. They're calling you *a bright and promising new face on the country music scene.*"

"Yeah, well, it was going really well. Until last night, that is..."

Webb leaned forward, concern evident on his face. "Elle, what's going on? Are you all right?"

"Well, my voice...it cracked last night. Right on the highest, loudest note. It was so humiliating. I started feeling afraid to go for the big notes.

I guess all the late nights and early mornings are taking a toll on my voice."

"Yeah, that would definitely do a number on your head. Especially singing in front of such huge crowds. But don't stress too much. Do you have your vocal exercises on your phone? The warm-ups and cooldowns?"

"Yeah, but...I guess I've been kind of lazy about using them."

"Well, maybe that's part of the problem. You got some Throat Coat tea out there? Everybody swears by it."

"Yeah, they always have it in catering."

"Listen. For the rest of the day take it easy. Don't talk. Be easy on your voice. Drink lots of water and all of that. At soundcheck, tell the sound guy that you're trying to let your voice rest up for tonight. He'll understand. After the show, go straight to bed and try to get a good night's sleep. "

"Yeah, that's what Blaine said to do too."

"Blaine Wesley, the bass player?"

"Yeah, that's him," Elle answered. "He's really good and such a great guy."

"He's an awesome bass player. Pretty sweet that he landed that tour."

Elle heard a voice say, "We're ready for you, buddy," and Webb said, "I'm gonna have to go, but I'm glad we talked."

"Me too." Elle waved to him as his face froze on the screen.

She couldn't put her finger on it, but something about the way Webb looked when she talked about Blaine gave her a weird feeling in the pit of her stomach.

Webb seemed jealous. What was all that about?

When Elle hung up, she saw that her dad had called earlier. Probably while she was in the shower. She figured he'd heard about the big "crack" last night. Becoming a record-company owner and CEO had infused him with a new sense of purpose after the death of Elle's mom nearly three years earlier.

Elle called him back. She knew he'd want to discuss her new single, but she really didn't want to get into it right now.

"Hi, darling. You're up early," he said.

"Hi, Daddy. Yeah, the bus rolled in not too long ago."

"Where are you today?"

"Today is Birmingham."

"Oh, that's right. And then Memphis?"

"Yep, that's right." She suppressed a yawn before she went on. "I thought I'd call you before I take a walk around downtown. I know you're getting the market-testing results today."

"Yep, today is the day."

Elle cleared her throat and coughed a couple of times.

"Elle, are you getting sick? Your voice sounds a bit hoarse."

"I'll be okay. I just wanted to say that even if the testing doesn't come back strong, I know 'Breakdown' is the right song to single."

"How about you let us worry about that? Go get some rest, and I'll let you know what the testing says. Everything will be fine."

Elle said nothing. She knew when he was talking down to her. He wanted her to back off.

"It's my career, Daddy. I'm the one who has to be on the road, singing these songs. I think my opinion should count for something."

"Don't worry, sweetheart. It'll all be fine. Now, you go get some rest."

Elle knew the conversation was over. She could hear voices in the background on his end. He was back in business mode. Daddy mode was over.

She wanted to tell him how exhausted she was and how scared she was of losing her voice in front of thousands of fans. But that was something you couldn't tell your label president.

"Okay, Daddy. But promise me you'll take my wishes into consideration."

"Sure, sweetie. Gotta go. Bye."

Elle hung up and tossed the phone into her purse a little harder than she'd meant to. Her dad infuriated her when he dismissed her. She knew she had to keep her cool, but her dad knew how to push all her buttons.

Before soundcheck Elle walked down one of the streets near the arena and headed into a café. She felt like having a chai latte, though she knew caffeine and milk were no-no's for her voice. She hadn't had one in so long, and she hated the way the Throat Coat tea tasted. She wanted something to make her feel better. And maybe something sweet to eat. She looked at the case of baked goods. One cream-cheese Danish had a ton of calories, but her soul needed a little nurturing. Catering was always so healthy. She could afford to splurge once in a while. Couldn't she?

Five

fter Elle left the café, she decided to take a tour of the Birmingham Civil Rights Institute in the town square.

As she sat on a bench outside the museum, waiting for it to open, she took in the spring morning air, sipping her chai latte and enjoying the last few bites of her Danish.

She noticed a scruffy man wearing a wrinkled T-shirt that had a huge picture of a Confederate flag across the front, along with the words *The South is Gonna Rise Again.*

Elle shook her head. What kind of a person would wear that shirt so close to the entrance of a civil rights museum? she wondered. The rebel flag represented the part of the south that had fought for slavery to remain legal. Elle's blood boiled just thinking about it.

A young African-American woman with two little girls walked past him on their way to the museum. The young woman's pretty pink jeans and white sweater matched the pink-and-white dresses both girls wore.

When they got within a few feet of the man, he yelled, "Hey, why you want to go learn a bunch of lies about a bunch of no-account ni—"

Elle sprang to her feet and stood in front of the man, her fists clenched. Then she raised her voice, hoping to drown out the awful word he had started to say.

"Back off! No one wants to hear what you have to say!"

He looked shocked, and then his eyes grew large. She could see hate in them. He grabbed Elle, and she started screaming for him to let her go.

She got in a good swift knee to his crotch, and the redneck collapsed in a heap on the sidewalk, moaning in pain just as a patrol car rolled up.

One cop made him stand and got him into the patrol car. Another police officer asked her what had happened. When Elle told him, he shook his head and said, "Always a nut job hanging around here."

Elle's throat ached from screaming. That couldn't be good.

The young mother came over and gave Elle a hug. "Thank you," she said. "That took a lot of courage."

The girls also hugged Elle. They said their goodbyes, and Elle walked away, feeling an odd mixture of happiness and exhaustion. She'd done a good thing, but her voice was going to suffer. And after the incident with the redneck, she no longer felt like touring the museum. She just wanted to get back to the hotel.

Elle stopped in a drugstore on the way back to pick up a few things she needed. Some candy bars were on sale, three for two dollars. She bought six and planned on sharing them with the band. They were such a good deal, how could she resist?

*   *   *

It had been a tough morning, and now, at sound-check, her voice was scratchier than ever. Her throat felt raw, and she didn't have the power she usually had. Every time she reached for a high note, it felt like her voice would tighten up and just vanish.

Blaine asked, "Elle, you okay?" He pointed to his throat. "How's it feeling?"

"Not good."

He nodded and then walked over and whispered something in Simon's ear.

"Okay, Elle. Now don't freak out, but I want to make a suggestion. On the big tours like this, where there is so much riding on each show, the risk of a singer losing his or her voice is pretty high. So the tour takes out a little insurance to make sure everyone can deliver."

"What are you saying, Blaine?"

He got a thumbs-up from Simon, who was turning knobs furiously at the sound board.

"Okay, Elle. Just sing, and if you think there's a note you're not going to be able to make, give Simon a sign, like two fingers behind your back, and watch what happens."

Elle was confused but curious. Blaine gave the band the count off and started into a song that Elle knew was going to be a challenge. As she was going for the high note at the top of the chorus, she put two fingers behind her back, and like magic, there was her voice, soaring gloriously up to the note. It sounded effortless. Then she realized she wasn't singing, yet her voice was booming over the sound system.

She waved her arms at the band. "Stop, stop stop!" She looked at Blaine and then at Simon. "What just happened? How did you do that?"

Simon came over and huddled around her with Blaine.

"All I did was turn the faders from your live voice down and turn the faders from the recording up. It's still you singing—with a little help."

Even though Elle was relieved to have a safety net, it also felt dishonest. It wasn't very "true blue."

She wasn't sure what to do. She could risk humiliating herself, possibly even losing the tour, or trade in her integrity and cheat.

Both options left her feeling sick to her stomach. If only she hadn't yelled at that stupid redneck. She buried her head in her hands. Then she ran back to her dressing room to hide and avoid the decision she knew she had to make.

Six

She huddled in a corner in the dark, clinging to her favorite pillow and wanting her mom. She wiped away the tears running down her cheeks. This wasn't at all what she had imagined her shot at the big time would be like. She closed her eyes and tried to calm herself. She wondered what her mother would say if she were here.

Her mind raced as she thought about all the shows coming up. The next day, Memphis. Two days later, Los Angeles—a show that everyone was saying would be attended by press, media and a lot of celebrities, including Johnny James's wife, Holly. Even if Elle could get through tonight's show without help, how would she get through Memphis? Then Los Angeles? Her stomach was in knots, and the room seemed to spin.

When she heard the knock on her door, she sat up a bit, wiped her tears and blew her nose. "Come in," she said, thinking it was probably Blaine coming to check on her.

The door cracked open, and she saw the outline of a cowboy hat. Her eyes widened as Johnny James peeked in at her.

"Hey, girl. You okay?" A surge of embarrassment and horror flooded her. Word had obviously spread fast about Elle's run-in with the redneck. Elle had been so emotional when she finally got back from downtown, she'd confided in Todd. He'd been so impressed by her courage that he'd told everyone what had happened.

Johnny walked over to her and got down on one knee. "Hey, don't beat yourself up now. Everybody goes through this when they start touring in the big leagues. The pressure..." He let out a long breath. "It's huge. And, well, we're only human, ya know? But the people, the fans, they want to see a great show. And we gotta give it to 'em."

Elle realized what he was telling her, even though he didn't say anything more. He patted her on the cheek, his hand lingering there for a moment. Then he winked, stood up and walked out of the dressing room.

The boss had spoken. Elle knew what she had to do.

True blue or not, the show must go on.

After Johnny left, Elle stayed huddled in the corner of her dressing room, her stomach churning. Maybe people in the entertainment world wouldn't call it cheating, but it certainly felt like that to her.

Her phone buzzed, alerting her to an email from Tommy, her A&R guy. He was the only person at the label other than her who wanted to single "Breakdown."

His message read, *I thought you'd want to know about this.* Below was an email from her father.

Hello, team,

I have considered all of your input from our meeting today on whether or not we should move forward with singling "Breakdown." There are insufficient findings to support releasing this song as a single.

Please let me know what other songs from the EP you feel would be strong candidates for testing for the next single.

Regards,
Steven Adams
President & CEO, Starstruck Records

Elle read it, sighed and immediately called Tommy. He picked up on the first ring.

"Sorry about sending that while you're on the road. I just thought you oughta know."

"Thanks, Tommy. I talked to my dad this morning, but he didn't mention it. To be honest, I can't believe he didn't tell me himself first."

"I know. That's gotta be tough. Listen, I know you couldn't be at the meeting, so I took the liberty of having my assistant type out what was said. I'm not sure it will make a big difference in the outcome, but at least you'll be informed a bit more about the process."

"I really appreciate your doing that," Elle said. "And yeah, I don't want to just stick my head in the sand. If I'm ever going to be successful in the music business, I need to have a basic under-standing of how it all works."

"I agree."

"There's time for him to reconsider, isn't there?" she asked. "Don't count 'Breakdown' out yet."

"I'll see what I can do," Tommy said. "Gotta go. Take care."

Elle sighed as she hung up the phone.

She had a sudden craving for something sweet and comforting. She remembered the candy bars she had bought when she stopped into the drugstore earlier that day.

She opened up her purse.

She only meant to eat one. She felt sick a few minutes later when she looked down at three wrappers lying on the floor.

Guilt washed over her. What was she doing? She locked her dressing-room door, walked to the washroom and made herself throw up.

Seven

Elle rolled out of her bunk on the bus later than usual the next day. The night before had been rough. She had done what she had to do. In almost every song she sang, there had come a moment when she had to give the signal to Simon. In the end, she guessed there was no harm done, but she tossed around in her bunk for hours after the show, unable to get to sleep.

She got dressed, grabbed her backpack and found her hotel key on the table of the front lounge. Attached to her hotel key was a sticky note from Todd. *Be back at the venue today by 12:30. Something special for lunch.*

She groaned and looked at her iPhone. It was already ten. That would only give her enough time to shower and get ready. She'd been hoping to skip lunch at the venue and take a nap until soundcheck at four. She sent Todd a text.

Got your note—needing some time for a nap at the room. Could I just come at soundcheck and skip lunch?

He wrote back, **Sorry, Elle, afraid not—something special planned for today at lunch. Need you here.**

She shook her head and texted back **fine.** The last thing she wanted to do was hang out with the band and crew.

She dragged herself off the bus and up to the hotel room, hoping to grab a quick nap before she showered.

When her cell phone rang in the elevator, her dad's face popped up on the screen. In all the chaos of the day before, she had totally forgotten to call and talk him out of killing "Breakdown."

Either he didn't understand or he didn't care how important the song was to her. She had told him that it represented how close she had come to breaking down and losing herself. Elle wanted her single to say something important about her own life. She wanted to be vulnerable and honest. Wasn't that what made people connect with an artist?

She picked up reluctantly. "Hey."

"Hey, darlin'. How's your voice?"

"Fine."

"Well, I hope it's better than fine. I don't have to remind you how important this tour is, do I?"

"No, Daddy, you have made that very clear."

"Good. There's a lot riding on your making a big impression on that tour."

"I know," Elle said, barely able to keep her voice steady.

"So, Elle, the testing wasn't as good as we'd hoped for 'Breakdown.' We're not going with it for a single."

Elle could feel her heart starting to pound. But she managed to contain her anger until she got into her room. No way did she want someone from the tour overhearing her fight with her dad.

"Yeah, Tommy told me. Was there any good feedback?" she asked, her voice sharp.

"Well, it wasn't all bad, but it's a risk, Elle, and not one I am willing to take."

"But Dad, I have this gut feeling—"

"Gut feelings don't sell records or pay $50,000 to single a song. We're going with a different song, and that's final!"

She was so mad she wanted to swear at him. Instead she pushed *end call*, flung her phone across the room and collapsed on the bed in tears.

She had never hung up on her father before. But she knew if she hadn't, she would have said something she would regret.

Her throat ached from crying. She sat up and wiped the hot tears off her face.

Then she climbed under the crisp white sheets and the goose-down duvet and opened the attachment on Tommy's email.

His assistant had done an amazing job of giving a detailed account of the meeting. Elle almost felt she was there.

She could see Jamie, the head of radio, at the top of the conference-room table, writing down the numbers from the testing on a whiteboard.

Elle knew it wasn't cheap to do radio testing. But these days, labels wouldn't even consider releasing a single without having testing done first. Like politicians taking a poll, labels had become totally dependent on the views of a handful of individuals who represented "the people."

A song was graded on a scale of one (low) to seven (high). The highest ranking of seven was rarely, if ever, achieved. But songs that tested between four and five were almost guaranteed to go on to radio success. Test groups were diverse—from teens to businessmen to stay-at-home moms and grandmas. The results were taken very seriously. All number-one singles in the past few years had scored between four and five in the test group.

Songs charting between six and ten made a lot of money. But artists dreamed of being in the top five because songs charting at numbers two, three, four and five received the same number of spins as the number-one song. That meant *big* money. Six-figures money. The number-one song was great bragging rights, but everyone knew that the song with the number-five slot was earning as much as the number-one song. Top five was the dream. Number one was just gravy.

The assistant's notes read:

Jamie wrote down stats based on the age, race and sex of those in the testing. He did not write down comments, positive or negative. He wrote down individual rankings of the song. It was hard to tell how the song had done.

Steven Adams: So what's the verdict?

Jamie: As you can see, "Breakdown" ranked high among the younger audience—five out of five females gave it a 5 to 6.5 ranking, with lots of positive comments. Like this one from a 25-year-old in Daytona Beach, Florida, who said, "I can so relate to this song—it's exactly what I wish I could say about what I'm going through." Or this 23-year-old girl from Los Angeles who gave it a 6.5 ranking and said, "The best song I've heard in years, and her voice is amazing!"

But then you turn to our middle-aged guys in the testing. They gave it a lower ranking of 3 to 3.5, with comments like "too mushy for me but her voice is impressive." Among middle-aged to older women, it ranked only fair—a 3.9 with some kind of neutral comments about the song. But they all seem to agree they like the sound of her voice.

Steven Adams: So what does all of this average out to?

Jamie: That's the tricky part. Calculations put it at a 3.9999, so we're right on the line.

Steven Adams: Tommy, what do you think?

Tommy: I think it's a strong song, and I know it means a lot to Elle. I vote yes.

Steven Adams: What about you, Grant?

Elle could picture Grant the marketing guy in his designer shirt and designer jeans with a little too much bling on the back pockets. Gross.

Grant: It isn't sexy. It's kind of a downer. I think the market is looking for something hotter. Something that's a bit more fun or aggressive and sexier will sell more.

Steven Adams: Jamie, what's your vote?

Jamie: Well...it's a bit of a gamble. On one hand, it ranked higher with the younger demographic than any song we've had in the last year, but the rest seem to be on the fence. I could go either way. Honestly, it could be a big hit or not do much. I just don't know.

Elle sat up against the headboard and wished she was somewhere else, doing anything else.

Why couldn't they just trust her? Trust Tommy?

Tommy had always believed that art drove commerce, but recently that had been turned on its ear. Music decisions were made by noncreatives who wanted a guarantee. A formula. The business side now ruled the creative process. But Tommy believed that things of an emotional and creative nature could not always be measured or ranked. Or guaranteed. Sometimes a risk had to be taken.

Almost all of Tommy's instincts had paid off with chart-topping singles. But the team around him had changed. This new team ruled with their heads instead of their hearts.

"Breakdown" wasn't just another song to Elle—it was personal. It had meaning on so many levels for her. Now it was as if her voice was being silenced once again. By someone who should want more than anything to hear her story.

Her father was looking out for what was good for the business. Not good for Elle.

What could she do? He was the boss.

A text message from Tommy popped up on her screen.

Don't give up on Breakdown yet. Marsha and I have an idea ☺

Eight

When Elle got to the catering tables, the twins were already working at being the center of attention. They were wearing skimpy little shorts and tank tops and flirting with the band. Elle had overheard Blaine and Todd talking about the twins in the back lounge of the bus. Most of the guys were married men. Their wives weren't too keen on the twins' behavior.

Elle did her best to steer clear of them, but they came up right behind her in the line for catering. "Where you been?" Mel asked.

Before Elle could reply, Shelly said, "By the way, Elle, your vocals sounded amazing last night!" She looked over at her sister and smirked. "It was so perfect, I thought it was the record."

The twins cackled. Elle felt sweat trickle down her back. Everyone on the tour must know she had used the recorded vocal to cheat. The twins had no idea what singing lead was like. The pressure.

As they sauntered out of catering, giggling and twitching their butts, Blaine came up behind her.

"Hey, don't pay any attention to them. They're just jealous of you and your talent. Not to mention how beautiful you are." His eyes met hers briefly. Then he looked over her shoulder and said, "Well, looks like you've got a visitor."

"Me?"

"Yep." He pointed toward the door.

Elle spun around and caught her breath. "Webb! What are you doing here?"

Several of the band guys called out, "Hey, Webb!" Everyone except the guitarist, Jack, liked Webb's music. Blaine walked over to shake his hand.

So *this* was Todd's lunch surprise.

Elle ran over and gave him a huge hug. She had never been more glad to see anyone after the day she'd had.

"Surprise!" Webb said. "I was hoping I could take you to lunch before soundcheck. I know about this awesome place Memphis is famous for. And I might have a few other sights for us to see. After all, when in Memphis..." He curled his lip and did an impressive Elvis impersonation.

Elle laughed for the first time in days—maybe weeks. She was so glad Webb was here. "But wait," she said. "You don't have a car."

"I do now."

Webb told Elle that Harley had decided to buy a new truck. He'd just received a big royalty check for his latest number-one song. "He met me for breakfast a couple of days ago and gave me the keys to his old truck and said, *Happy birthday, whenever your birthday is.* I tried to refuse, but he insisted...so I have wheels!"

Elle gave him a high five.

* * *

They drove with the windows down, Elvis tunes filling the air.

Elle looked over at Webb. He was grinning, his tanned hands gripping the steering wheel of his black Ford F-150. He had never looked so good to her.

The GPS guided them to their destination. Soon Elle and Webb were standing on the hallowed floor of Sun Studio.

Elle knew that back in the early 1950s, a white man named Sam Phillips had been determined to bring African-American music to white audiences.

"It's hard to believe that all those life-changing sounds began in this studio. Elvis Presley, Howlin' Wolf, B.B. King..." Webb said.

Gold and platinum records took up every square inch of space in the small lobby. A narrow hallway led back to a control room. A vintage soundboard looked onto a small tracking room through a large square window. The window allowed the people in the control booth to see the performers.

In the tracking room stood a single mic on a stand, a vintage red drum set and a couple of old Gibson guitars. The mic looked like the ones Elle used to see at the Grand Ole Opry. The tracking booth looked like a glorified closet. The hardwood floors were scuffed. Elle imagined a singer pacing, trying to get the vocals right. Back when singing live was what separated the pretenders from the real deals.

All those legends had struggled to maintain artistic integrity. Especially people like Johnny Cash. He did things his way and didn't much care who got mad.

Webb looked as if he were standing on sacred ground.

"Can you imagine what it took for those artists to stay true to themselves? It inspires me! I want to be like that. Stay real. Never sell out. Even if I never make it big."

Elle was reminded of what had happened the night before during the show. Was she selling out? Or was she being a professional?

After leaving the studio, they had a little time to walk down Beale Street, looking in the windows of the famous blues clubs. Most of them were closed this early in the day. A couple were open for the lunch crowd. They could hear the soulful sound of a blues guitar playing softly over tinkling glasses and conversation.

Entering the Orpheum Theater was like stepping back in time. It almost took her breath away. The seats were cushioned in deep-red velvet. When she looked up, she saw golden ceilings with ornate moldings and detailed drawings.

It would be amazing to stand on this stage and sing.

An alarm went off on Webb's phone. "Time for lunch," he said.

"You set an alarm?"

"Yep. Gotta get you something to eat and then have you back for soundcheck. Mr. Todd runs a tight ship."

He put his hand behind her back and guided her down the street to what looked to be a small dive with a sign that read *Rendezvous Ribs*.

"This place is the most famous rib place in the entire south," Webb said. "The Rolling Stones used to have Rendezvous ribs flown out to shows when they were craving them."

Elle felt ravenous when the ribs arrived but was careful not to attack the rack of ribs in front of Webb. She had to look good in her dress tonight. A big meal could change all that.

Webb pulled a small gift bag out of his jacket pocket. "I brought you a little something to remind you of Nashville."

With a tentative smile, he handed her the package. Elle took the gift bag in her hands.

It was from one of her favorite shops—Fanny's House of Music, which sold music equipment and vintage clothing.

"Go ahead and open it," Webb said.

She untied the burlap twine and opened the teal-blue wrapping.

"Oh, Webb, it's beautiful." She held up a vintage scarf in shades of teal and brown and yellow. "I love it!"

"Thought it would look great in your hair," Webb said.

She blushed and wondered why she suddenly felt so shy.

While they ate she told Webb about her dad's decision not to single "Breakdown."

"Tommy sent me the notes from the meeting. He thinks my dad's making the wrong decision too."

"I'm sorry, Elle," Webb said. "'Breakdown' is such a great song." He shook his head. "At least you have Tommy on your side."

"Yep. And Tommy and Marsha might even have something up their sleeves, but I guess we'll have to wait and see what happens."

Another alarm sounded on Webb's phone. "Time flies. Got to get you back to soundcheck."

Elle couldn't think of anything she wanted to do less.

Nine

They arrived back from lunch just in time for soundcheck. Elle left Webb backstage and went to her dressing room to get ready.

All that talk with Webb about artistic integrity had made Elle feel very nervous about the show. And about what she'd done the night before. Cheat.

But did she have a choice?

Johnny James had practically ordered her to do whatever it took not to ruin the show. And now Webb was here for the show, and he'd find out just how fake she was! What was she going to do?

She knew how much being authentic meant to Webb. If he stayed for the show, he would lose all respect for her. She had to think of a way to get him to leave.

She closed her eyes and said a prayer for help. When she reached the edge of the stage, she saw Jack and Shel pawing each other. *Disgusting*.

Then it came to her. She knew what she had to do. She walked straight past Webb and over to Blaine, giving him her full attention. Smiling up at him. Touching his arm as she talked about Beale Street and how much she thought he would love it. Blaine seemed to be thoroughly enjoying himself, but it was clear someone else was not.

Webb was standing offstage, watching her and Blaine. He was frowning. But would it be enough?

Soundcheck continued. Elle didn't sing very much. She needed to save her voice. But in the middle of one of the songs, she went over and danced with Blaine. She let her hips sway to the beat as he played.

After soundcheck she walked off the stage, her arm linked in Blaine's. She waved goodbye to Webb as though she didn't have the time of day for him.

"Elle, what's going on?" Blaine said. "You just walked past Webb without speaking to him. And what's with all the PDA?"

"Just play along, will you?" she said through a fake smile.

"No, Elle. You can find someone else to play games with."

He slipped his arm from hers and walked back to the band dressing room.

She locked eyes with Webb for a second before he turned and walked out. She could tell he was mad. She wanted to run after him, but if she did, she would tell him everything. She couldn't risk losing him and his respect. It was better this way.

Back in her dressing room, Elle took a deep breath and told herself to get it together. She managed to put on her makeup and put some loose curls in her hair. She started zipping up her dress and had to breath in a little to get it to zip. Definitely too many ribs at lunch. Elle pushed the thought out of her mind. Nothing she could do about that now. She took the beautiful vintage scarf out of the bag and tied it in her hair. It matched her dress perfectly, and she felt better wearing it. It was almost like having Webb there. She hoped he wasn't too mad. He was probably on his way back to Nashville. She would text him after her set and apologize for the whole Blaine thing. Though she had no idea what she would say.

* * *

Before the real show started, the lights dimmed and two local DJs came out and gave away tickets to the Bahamas and made lame jokes. It felt to Elle like they'd never get off the stage.

Finally they got to Elle's intro. "Ladies and gentlemen, would you please give a warm Memphis welcome to the up-and-coming country artist Nashville is buzzing about. Starstruck Records national recording artist Elle!!!!!!"

The crowd seemed genuinely excited, and their applause was more than polite.

The encouragement gave Elle the adrenaline boost she needed. Who was she kidding? Singing and performing came as naturally to Elle as breathing. She was a couple of songs into the set, and she had not had to cheat. Her voice, live and in person, and nothing else.

She set up for "Breakdown." It used to be the part of her set she most looked forward to. But it was vocally challenging, and now she dreaded it.

"This is for anyone out there who's ever felt alone. You're not the only one," she said.

Elle started singing. It was mesmerizing. It was quiet enough in the huge venue to hear a pin drop. Her voice was a little raspy, but that just added to the emotion. For a while Elle was lost in the music. The audience seemed to be completely enthralled.

People were taking pictures and shooting videos. Then Elle became aware of a guy in the front row who was doing something alarming.

He was undressing.

At first he just took off his jacket. But then his shirt came off and then his pants. Security rushed in to whisk him away. Anyone who could see what was going on was distracted. So was Elle. She had heard there were some freaky fans out there, but this was the first time she had ever seen something like this.

She was losing focus. Losing her confidence. She braced herself for the high note in the song's bridge. It would be a challenge for any singer in her best voice. Elle knew she couldn't reach it.

And yet she seemed to float effortlessly up to the note. Just like the recording! It was incredible.

But then she started to cough, and for a couple of seconds her voice kept going while she turned her head off the mic.

The audience started to boo. Elle closed her eyes and stopped singing. Simon, thank goodness, was able to stop the recorded vocal, but the damage was done. Elle glanced over at Blaine, who had a look of absolute panic on his face.

Then someone yelled out, "Faker!"

"Nice lip-synching."

"We thought you could really sing!"

"Get off the stage!"

Elle stood there for a few minutes, feeling their hate. Could these be the same people who had loved her earlier in the show?

Finally she broke out of her trance and ran off the stage.

Johnny James's band was standing backstage in a circle, shaking their heads. Then Todd said, "Get out there, boys! Go play some Elvis songs. Twins, you ready to sing?" Shel and Mel nodded. Within minutes, the band and the twins had the crowd on their feet with some salutes to Elvis and B.B. King.

Elle escaped to her dressing room. She had caught a glimpse of Johnny James out of the corner of her eye as she ran from the stage. He looked to be reaming out Simon.

This was not good. Not good for Elle. Not good for the tour. Not good for Simon. Not good for Starstruck Records.

Someone knocked on her door.

It was probably Todd. How could she face him? The knock came again.

She got up and opened the door, her mascara running down her face through her tears.

There in front of her was Webb, holding a dozen pink roses. And the look on his face wasn't judgment. It was compassion. And something else.

She fell into his arms just before she fainted.

Ten

Todd called Elle's father immediately after he found out that Elle had fainted.

There were paramedics at every venue. When they came to the dressing room and examined Elle, they recommended she be taken to Memphis General. Elle's father asked them to wait a few minutes to see if she stabilized. "He said the last thing we need is rumors about her health getting out," Todd said.

Elle nodded. She was groggy but aware of what was going on. She didn't need some gossip rag saying she'd overdosed.

Webb said, "I can take her to the hospital, Todd. Then I'll drive her back to Nashville when they release her. No one will follow us."

Todd looked unsure. "Mr. Adams—"

"Tell him I'll call him later. We have to think of Elle first."

Finally Todd agreed. Webb asked the paramedics to help him get Elle to his truck and then slowly drove her to the hospital.

She drifted in and out of sleep as they drove the twenty minutes to the ER.

They checked her heart, her vital signs, her blood. Everything seemed fine, other than her cholesterol being slightly elevated. Elle wondered if that was thanks to the lunch at Rendezvous Ribs. In the end, she was diagnosed with fatigue-and-stress-related fainting. Not that surprising, really. All she needed was *rest and no stress.* As if.

When the doctor discharged her the next morning, Elle and Webb drove back to Nashville. The scandal of the young country singer who had been caught lip-synching was all over the news. Apparently, it was all over YouTube too. Maybe her career was over. Maybe she'd have to busk for a living. Elle closed her eyes and tried to sleep.

* * *

"Bernie and I have been talking to Johnny's people," her dad said the morning after she arrived back in Nashville. She was still in bed, but her dad had set up a conference call. "Bernie's here, and Lesley, and Johnny's manager, Beau. I want you to listen, but you are not to speak. Understood?"

Elle nodded. She didn't like to be told when she could and couldn't speak. But she also didn't want to talk about what had happened. She was happy to listen. This time.

"The immediate issue is the Los Angeles show at the Staples Center in three days. Probably the biggest show of the tour," Bernie piped in.

"It's not lost on us that this kind of publicity is a very good opportunity to bring out the press." Bernie could spin anything, even this latest disaster. "Listen, there's gonna be a feeding frenzy about Elle, but hey, even bad press is press," he continued. "There's blood in the water, and the media sharks are circling. It's make-or-break time."

"Can I say something, gentlemen?" Lesley, the tour publicist, said.

"Yes, please," said Beau, a soft-spoken man who was well respected in the music business.

"Do you know what the media loves more than anything?" Lesley said. "What the *people* love more than anything? A comeback story! We just need to create a story about the difficulty Elle has faced, her personal struggle. If we spin it that way, everyone will *love* it."

The men all agreed, and Bernie said, "While you're working on that, maybe we should get her into one of those LA vocal coaches. Get her whipped into shape in no time. I hear they can do miracles!"

"Great idea, Bernie!" her father said.

"I know someone in LA that could get us in with Louis Lamont, vocal guru to the stars," Bernie said. "If you guys can get her on a plane to Los Angeles first thing in the morning, I'll get her in with Louis tomorrow afternoon. Maybe have a second session the following morning. She'll be ready for the Staples show."

Everyone agreed to that plan of action. Elle didn't say a word.

* * *

Her father called her after the conference call and told her he'd have his assistant book Elle's flight to LA. He didn't even mention what had happened in Memphis. It was as if he couldn't process it. "Bernie's offered to come with you," he said.

"No way!" Elle replied. "I am not sitting beside him on a plane for four hours. You know how I feel about him. Please, Dad. Someone else. Anyone else."

Her dad blew a long breath out. "Who do you want to take you then? I'd go myself, but there's simply too much damage control to do in Nashville."

The answer was easy. "Webb."

"Fine. I'll get Tanya to book two flights and two hotel rooms. You're lucky to have a friend like Webb."

"I know," Elle said.

Eleven

"**W**elcome to Los Angeles. The local time is 9:00 AM Pacific Standard Time."

Because Tanya had booked them in the first row of first class, they were the first off the plane.

The California breeze was dry and warm. If Elle hadn't been nauseous since the Memphis show, she might have been able to enjoy this trip. Might even have been excited about it. As it was, a dark cloud hung over her, and she couldn't stop thinking about the show in two days at the Staples Center.

She and Webb made their way to the baggage-claim area, grabbed their bags off the carousel and found a driver holding up a sign that said *Starstruck Records*.

They followed him to a black SUV. As they drove into the city, Elle looked out the window, amazed at the eight lanes of traffic on the freeway. Everyone was going so fast. There were ramps and exits everywhere. It all made her feel dizzy.

She was a long way from her small hometown in Minnesota.

They reached the hotel in about forty minutes. The driver said they were lucky that traffic going into Beverly Hills was very light at this time of day. Elle couldn't imagine what rush hour would be like.

Webb started telling Elle all about the history of the Beverly Hilton, where her dad had arranged for them to stay. The grand International Ballroom was where the Golden Globes had been held for decades. Angelina Jolie had vowed to jump in the pool in her ball gown if she won a Golden Globe for her role in *Gia*. She won and kept her promise. Clive Davis, one of Hollywood's most famous record executives, hosted his yearly Grammy party at the Beverly Hilton. The most recent event that had put the Beverly Hilton in the news was Whitney Houston's death in her suite on the day of the annual Grammy party.

LA was a weird town, Elle thought. But you had to love the feeling of possibility in the air. And the weather. Sunny skies and no rain, every day.

Elle noticed how many beautiful people there were everywhere. The woman who checked them in at the hotel was stunning. The bellhop who carried their bags to their rooms was super hot. ("Don't even think of carrying your own bags in LA. They live on tips," Webb told her.) Even the wait staff at lunch were gorgeous. Clearly, everyone was waiting for his or her big break. How many of them would succeed? If it was anything like Nashville, not very many. She was one of the lucky ones. And look where she'd ended up.

She and Webb looked a bit out of place in their Nashville casual attire—faded jeans, plaid shirts and cowboy boots—but it made Elle appreciate her life in Nashville a little more. At least she didn't have to try and compete in this rat race.

She heard the sound of a camera shutter behind her. Paparazzi. She'd heard about them, but she wasn't on anyone's radar. Elle looked around for somebody famous.

A short squat man with a Trump-like comb-over was snapping photos of her and Webb, not some random celebrity.

"Elle, how's the voice?" the guy yelled.

Webb took over, shielding her and walking briskly into the hotel. In the lobby there was another man waiting, camera ready.

Word had spread. The media were out for blood.

Elle fought back angry tears as Webb put his arm around her and walked her quickly through the lobby.

"How did they find us?" she asked when they got to the hallway outside their rooms. No one else was around. "This is crazy."

He shook his head. "I don't know. Maybe someone tipped them off at the hotel. I guess what happened in Memphis was bigger than we thought. Johnny James and all. I'm sorry, Elle. You just gotta keep your head up. It's gonna be all right. The sharks will come and go, but you have true talent. You'll get through this." He looked down at his watch. "Okay. It's already one. We're due at the vocal coach's studio at three. Might give you time for a short nap."

Elle yawned at the thought of a nap. That would definitely help.

"How about we meet here at two thirty? The studio isn't very far away. I'll have an Uber pick us at the side entrance of the hotel. That way we can avoid the lobby."

"Sounds good." Without thinking about it, she reached up and gave him a kiss on the cheek. "Thank you, Webb. I don't think I could have survived the last few days without you."

He smiled. "That's what friends do."

She backed away from him into her room. Her heart was racing. What was happening?

Friends. Was that really how he thought of her? If it was true, she had to stop thinking it could be anything else. It would only end in heartbreak. She seemed to be feeling a lot of that these days.

Twelve

When they arrived at Louis Lamont's studio, they pushed through a bamboo gate into a garden that reminded Elle of Mr. Miyagi's garden in the original version of *The Karate Kid*.

The smog and traffic of LA disappeared as they stepped into a Zen garden with statues and waterfalls and the soft music of pan flutes playing over a hidden sound system.

Elle and Webb were greeted by a beautiful woman in a kimono. She bowed deeply.

"Welcome, welcome. Master Louis will see you. Right this way."

They followed her through the garden to where a deeply tanned man in a white loincloth was sitting in the lotus position in front of a statue of the Buddha.

They all stood in silence until the man took a deep breath and opened his eyes.

"Welcome, Elle. Welcome," he said. "And who are you?" he asked Webb.

His voice had a deep, unmistakable Southern twang. A strange mix with the loincloth and the Buddha. Elle said, "This is my friend Webb. He's a singer-songwriter too."

"Welcome to you both. If you will follow Michiko into the piano garden, I will meet you there shortly."

They followed her into a room that was like an indoor garden, with screens and a roof to protect the beautiful nine-foot mahogany grand piano. There were cushions on the floor in front of the piano, which put Elle's face at eye level with the piano bench.

When he returned, Louis was wearing a white linen tunic and loose white pants that floated around his bare feet. Instead of sitting on the bench, he sat on a floor cushion across from Elle. Webb scooted his pillow a few feet away.

Louis stared at Elle for a while before he said, "Now Elle—or may I call you E?"

The Southern accent was so strong that Elle could barely keep a straight face. *E?* What was that about?

"Breathe with me," Louis continued. "Breathe from deep in your core." He pronounced *core* as if it had two syllables—"co-ore."

"Pull all the air from your being. Air is the life of your voice, your song."

Elle did as he asked, feeling more than a little awkward. *What must Webb be thinking?*

"I sense that you have great chaos inside. You must find peace. Peace with your essence. Breath deep. Now reach high, E, and streeeeetch."

Louis took Elle through a series of yoga poses and deep-breathing exercises. After a while Elle looked over at Webb, wondering if he was thinking what she was. When was Southern Yoda going to get around to a voice lesson?

Then Louis rose to his feet and asked Elle to stand.

"Now, sing this with me." He sat at the piano and took her through a scale, reminding her to remember her essence, her inner peace. "You can never release your true voice without inner peace."

When her voice made a horrible cracking sound at the top of the scale, he was obviously concerned. "That is where your chaos is, E. You must release your chaos to free your voice. Try it again."

Elle could feel herself scowl as she tried to release her inner chaos and find her essence, or whatever Louis was trying to make her do. Her voice got worse, not better. Finally Louis stopped her.

"I believe I have an idea that will help you. We have so little time. I would like to invite a colleague of mine, a medical doctor, to assist me." He turned to his assistant. "Michiko! Please call Dr. Marong. Ask him to come at once!"

Michiko left the room, and Louis followed her.

Elle and Webb exchanged confused glances. What the heck had just happened? Webb pulled up Dr. Marong's website on his phone. The doctor's photo looked as if it had been done at a professional photo shoot. Only in LA.

Fifteen minutes later Louis sauntered in with a young man with a deep tan and long golden hair. He would have been at home on a surfboard. "This is Dr. Marong. He can give you a shot that will heal the damage to your vocal cords and give you the full use of your range. I recommend a shot today and one more tomorrow. This is only a temporary solution though. Dear E, you must find inner peace and discover your essence. Otherwise I am afraid this will be a recurring problem."

Elle wasn't so sure how she felt about a total stranger sticking a needle in her...wherever. Even if he was a Hollywood doctor to the stars. Webb asked if they could step out to discuss this for a few minutes.

"Certainly. Michiko will show you to the Quiet Garden."

When they were alone, Webb said, "Okay. I did a quick Google search on steroid shots for vocal problems, and it's true what he says. It will heal the damage for a while. But not forever. I don't know, Elle—it's your call. You're the one who's gonna be standing on that stage singing in front of thousands of fans. Maybe it's okay for that show, but beyond that...Maybe you should call your dad and ask what he thinks?"

Elle didn't need to call. She knew what Steven McAdams, CEO of Starstruck Records, would say. She said it now, lowering her voice to imitate him.

"Do whatever it takes, Elle. They are the experts. If they say you need a shot, then get the shot."

She took a deep breath and looked up at Webb. "I'm gonna do it. Then I want to get out of here."

Webb nodded, and they walked back to the piano room. Louis and the doctor were sipping something from tiny white mugs. Elle hoped it was tea.

The doctor gave her the shot—in her arm, thank goodness—and told her to come to his office the next day after lunch for a follow-up shot.

As she and Webb got into their Uber, she felt hungry again, even though they had eaten not long ago. Maybe it was her inner chaos that was making her want to eat. She knew she had to get a handle on that if she hoped to zip up the dress she had planned to wear for the LA show.

Maybe a jog along the beach in Santa Monica would help. Or a bike ride. Something to take her mind off all this craziness. When she told Webb her idea, his face totally lit up.

When they got back to the hotel, they changed into beach clothes and grabbed another Uber to the Santa Monica Pier.

They walked along the beach, talking about everything—music, life, their childhoods, Webb's adventures with his cousins.

They rented bikes and rode along the walkway, stopping for tacos before they watched the sunset at the pier.

She stood beside him as the warm glow of the sun melted into the ocean. She ached for him to take her in his arms. He turned and looked at her, their eyes locked, and then—

"Hey, buddy! Got a couple bucks for a guy down on his luck?" The golden moment passed. A guy who reminded Elle of the homeless man in Nashville named Johnny Cash stood in front of them with his hand out. Webb reached in his back pocket to dig out a few bucks.

"Where you from?" Webb asked.

"Dallas. Came down here to catch some waves and never went back," the man replied. "Can't beat the weather."

"Take care of yourself, man," Webb said. The man waved as he walked away.

They returned the bikes and Ubered back to the hotel. Elle was fighting a lump in her throat and butterflies in her stomach all the way. What was wrong with her? She looked over at Webb, and she knew the answer. She had feelings for him, and he thought of her as just a friend.

The show, Elle, she told herself. *Just think about the show.*

Thirteen

The next day was a blur. They checked out of the room at eleven, grabbed lunch, then Ubered to the doctor's office for Elle's second shot. Then it was off to the Staples Center for soundcheck. Elle's stomach was in knots. As she rounded a corner in the back-stage area, she found her stylists, Kara and Brian, taking a selfie with Johnny's wife, Holly. When Holly turned to walk away, Elle made eye contact with Kara and Brian, who stopped smiling and started frowning.

"What are you guys doing here?" Elle asked. "I thought you were back in Nashville."

"Do you think we would let you just wing it for the biggest show of the tour?" Kara said.

Brian stood behind Kara with his finger across his lips, nodding his head in agreement.

Kara continued, "We got a call from some amazing local designers who said they'd love for you to wear their pieces for the show tonight. Isn't that exciting!"

"Yeah, great." She didn't try to hide her lack of excitement. She wasn't surprised when Kara's temper flared.

"Look, Elle, I don't mind telling you, your little lip-synch blunder has gotten a lot of attention. In this business, even bad press is good press. This is a golden opportunity for you to extend some goodwill to the design community in LA."

Elle tried to stop herself from rolling her eyes but failed. Weary of arguing, she agreed to try on a couple of dresses.

She and Kara went to her dressing room. Elle put on an insanely short sequined dress. It looked like a figure skater's outfit. She stepped out from behind the divider to ask Kara to zip the dress up for her.

"Ahh...put on a few pounds, have you? I'm afraid to try and zip it to the top. I guess I assumed you'd be the same size as you were at the beginning of the tour."

Kara's words cut Elle to the quick, but she tried not to show it.

"Well, obviously I'm *not!*" Elle ducked behind the divider, threw the dress over to Kara and said, "On second thought, Kara, I'm sticking with the dress I planned to wear. Can you let yourself out?"

"But—"

"But nothing. See you. Bye-bye."

It felt good to tell Kara to take her stupid designer dresses and leave. Especially since it had been humiliating to have her weight gain pointed out.

Once she heard the door slam behind Kara, she looked down at herself in her underwear. So she'd put on a couple of pounds. What was the big deal? She was never going to be a size 0. And her fans didn't care, did they?

She would wear one of the three dresses she had already worn on the tour. And she'd tie Webb's scarf in her hair for good luck. She could use some about now.

*　*　*

Webb escorted Elle to the backstage area and then announced that he was going to the Museum of Contemporary Art for a while.

The guys in the band seemed happy to see her. Relieved even. She'd been worried about being around Blaine, but he was as friendly as ever.

Simon pulled Elle aside. "Elle, I'm so sorry about what happened in Memphis. I should have been watching more closely. I can't imagine how hard it's been."

Elle touched his arm. "It's not your fault. It's on me. But tonight I'm going with what I have. Win or lose, good or bad. I'm singing live—all the time."

She could see the immediate relief on Simon's face.

After soundcheck she went back to her dressing room to get ready for the show. The blue dress was a little snug, but it still fit. She looked in the mirror and wondered how crazy it was to test Dr. Marong's shot at such a big show. But it was the only way to go. She had to accept the gift even if it had come in a weird package.

She heard a knock on the door and the welcome sound of Webb's voice.

"Time to go. You ready?"

She took a deep breath. "As I'll ever be."

She had to let it happen and hope for the best.

When she reached for the notes, there they were. She had never experienced anything like it. It was almost scary, the instant gratification of having her voice returned to her.

Johnny James came out of his dressing room to watch Elle's entire set from the wings of the stage.

Dr. Marong had told her that steroid shots suppressed the immune system, so it was important for her to eat right and get lots of rest for the next several days. But right now, onstage and singing her heart out, she felt fantastic.

Louis and Dr. Marong came backstage after the show and gave her Euro kisses and big hugs, telling her how "simply fabulous" she had been.

Lesley had scheduled a press conference after the show. Elle was going to set the record straight about the whole Memphis fiasco.

The press met in the green room backstage.

Elle had no trouble fielding questions. Her confidence had been given a huge boost by her stellar performance. She felt like a total pro.

Elle's cell phone rang in the middle of the press conference. When she answered it, her dad said, "You did it! You pulled it off! Way to go, kiddo!"

"Thanks, Dad. But how do you know? You're not here."

"Oh, it's all over Twitter, Snapchat and Instagram how amazing you were. And Bernie and Lesley have been keeping me informed."

Elle was sure he had spies everywhere. She hung up quickly when she saw Johnny's wife, Holly, walking toward her with a couple of friends.

"You were amazing, Elle! Wasn't she?" She turned to her friends.

Elle tried not to geek out when she realized that Holly's friends were the stars of *Agents of S.H.I.E.L.D.*, one of her favorite TV shows.

Then Holly leaned in and whispered, "What happened in Memphis must have been awful. The media can be so horrid. You have true talent. Just take care of yourself, and don't let anybody push you around."

She gave Elle a warm hug, and for a moment Elle saw past the designer clothes and the famous friends. Holly knew what it was like to struggle. Johnny James was a lucky guy to have such an amazing wife.

Webb hung back, giving Elle all the space she needed to fully live in the moment. After everyone was gone, he was still there, waiting for Elle to gather her things so he could drive her to the airport hotel. They were to fly out to Nashville the next morning.

The Nashville show was in two days, and she was excited about it. As difficult as the criticism had been after Memphis, the praise she had just received had wiped all of that away.

Webb listened as she rambled on. When she finally took a breath and let a few moments of silence waft in the air, he began to speak.

"I'm stoked for how the show went tonight. It was amazing. I just want you to remember to take care of yourself for the next two days, especially before the Nashville show. Remember what the doc said. You gotta take care of yourself and your voice. Maybe you should be on vocal rest until the Nashville show. Lots of sleep tonight. No staying up late."

Elle sat in silence, wondering why Webb was being such a downer.

After a few minutes, Webb said, "Spit it out. What are you not saying?"

"I really wanted to celebrate with you."

"I'm sorry, Elle. I'm just trying to make sure that you're okay for the next show. Two steroid shots in two days can be tough on your immune system, that's all."

Elle looked out the window. Why couldn't they go and have some fun? She'd had enough stress to last a lifetime. But if he didn't want to be with her...

She knew Webb was right, of course.

She had talked too much after the show. Every singer knew that talking wears your voice out more than singing.

If she wasn't careful, the magical results of the steroid shots could disappear.

Maybe a midnight snack would help.

Fourteen

Her wake-up call came at six thirty the next morning. Elle had had trouble sleeping and ended up channel-surfing for hours. Now she was feeling seriously fatigued and a little chilled. Webb had a worried look on his face when the elevator doors opened and he saw her.

"You okay?"

"I'll be fine," was all she said.

Her voice sounded tired, even to her.

Webb said, "You can sleep all the way back to Nashville. That will help, right?"

"Yeah, sure." She just wanted to be in her own bed in her own apartment in Nashville. Life on the road was not so glamorous after all.

She slept on the flight, and Webb delivered her to her apartment after a silent ride from the airport. He didn't stay long. Were all the good feelings between them gone? Had they gotten lost in all the craziness?

Elle knew she was being horrible to Webb. She felt anchorless. Maybe she would feel better with more sleep. She knew she had to be sure she was rested for the show the next night.

What if the Nashville show wasn't as great? Then what?

The life of a performer was so up and down. If you had a great night, you were flying high, and everyone loved you. But if you had a bad night, you got criticized and were made to feel like a loser. You still had to plaster on a smile and go out and perform as if nothing bothered you.

What was it about performing that made it all worthwhile? Could she hold up vocally under this kind of pressure?

She had never had any sort of formal vocal training, and now she needed Dr. Marong's miraculous steroid shots. What did that say about her talent? And her authenticity?

Stressing out made her hungry. Pizza sounded good, but she had been advised against eating cheese. Dairy products created mucus on the vocal cords.

But the show wasn't until the next night. She'd be fine. The next thing she knew, a pizza-delivery guy was standing at her door with a large stuffed-crust pizza. She slipped the box onto her kitchen table. I'll eat two slices and put the rest in the fridge for later, she thought.

But once she started eating, she couldn't stop. She ate until there were only three slices left.

Almost immediately she felt mucus rising up in her throat. She spent the next thirty minutes hacking and coughing. An overload of dairy, grease and stomach acid was a recipe for disaster.

Her stomach felt like it was going to explode. How was she going to zip up her dress? It had already been feeling too snug in LA. She ran to the toilet and made herself throw up.

What was she doing?

She was never going to do that again. Never.

Her cell phone rang, and Marsha's face appeared on her screen. She couldn't pick up, not in the state she was in.

All she wanted to do was run five miles to prove she had everything under control. She let the call go to voice mail and then checked it.

Marsha's warm voice said, "Hey, Elle, thinking of you. Listen, I wanted to let you know that I'll be there tomorrow night with bells on. I also wanted to give you the number of my friend Beth. She's a fantastic vocal coach here in town. I thought if you wanted to see her, she might be able to give you a session before tomorrow night. Her number is 615-555-5656. She knows you might call and will make time to see you."

Elle put Beth's number in her phone. It couldn't hurt to call her, especially now that her throat was feeling rough after throwing up. She hadn't even thought about how stomach acid would affect her voice.

She called Beth and asked for an appointment.

"I have an opening in two hours," Beth said. "Would that work for you?"

"Two hours is perfect," Elle said. Then she threw on her running clothes, determined to sweat off whatever toxins she had put into her body.

"Get it together!" she kept telling herself as she ran. "It was only pizza."

Halfway through her run, her phone rang again. She answered it but kept running. Her dad would keep calling if she didn't answer.

"Hey, Dad."

"Hey, honey, you sound out of breath. Everything okay?"

"I'm on my run."

"Getting pumped up for the big show tomorrow night?"

"Yep."

"Okay, I won't keep you. Just wanted to let you know that everyone is really feeling good about singling 'Cowboy Baby.'"

Elle rolled her eyes. She hated that song and had only put it on the EP because the marketing team would not relent until she did.

"Dad, I didn't even write that song. It's so different from everything else on the EP. How about the song Marsha and I wrote? There are so many other good options. Can't we at least consider something else?"

"Look, Elle, Grant feels strongly about it, and Jamie thinks it could test strong."

"And what about Tommy? What does he say?"

"I haven't run it by Tommy yet. Grant just brought the idea in this morning. We had an unplanned meeting, and Tommy couldn't be there."

"I still think 'Breakdown' is the best to single."

"Give it up, Elle. That ship has sailed."

"Okay, Dad, I have to go. I'm back at my place, and I need to shower. I have a vocal session in forty-five minutes."

"Seems like Louis is something of a miracle worker."

Elle rolled her eyes again, thinking of Louis and all his spiritual mumbo jumbo. "Oh, he was something, all right."

"He certainly wasn't cheap, but it paid off, didn't it? The LA show was a total success!"

"Okay, Dad, I really have to go."

She hung up, fuming over the idea that "Cowboy Baby" would be her first single. It was as if Grant and Jamie had some sort of spell over her dad, making promises for success. She knew this was her dad's weak spot.

He was an overachiever, and, above everything else, he wanted to achieve success.

She wondered if she was a little like that too.

Her mom hadn't been like that at all. All she had wanted was a happy family. But there was no point in dwelling on her mom now. She had to focus on reality.

Which was that her dad was listening to all the wrong people.

Fifteen

After a quick shower, Elle screeched out of her parking garage and raced to her appointment. She would barely make it in time. When she saw the blue lights in her rear-view mirror, she swore. Getting pulled over for speeding was not what she needed right now. She shot Beth a quick text and waited for her lecture and her ticket.

When Elle finally arrived, Beth greeted her warmly. She was very attractive in an East Nashville bohemian sort of way. Her accent was faintly Southern, but her voice was deep and clear. Her loft studio was very inviting but simple. The tall windows let in lots of light. Her view overlooked a row of trees and a quiet sidewalk.

In the center of the studio was a small grand piano.

Beth invited Elle to sit in one of the two chairs in the studio so they could get acquainted.

"So, Elle, how is the tour going? How is your voice holding up? What kind of struggles have you been experiencing?"

Elle couldn't help herself. Beth seemed so sympathetic and down to earth. She spilled everything. Late nights on the bus. The rebel-flag guy in Birmingham. Her vocal issues. Johnny James basically telling her she had to deliver a great performance, whatever it took. The awful night in Memphis. Fainting after the show. She ended with her visit to Loco Louis in LA and Dr. Marong's shots.

Beth listened closely, asking additional questions about Dr. Marong and the shots. Elle felt exhausted but also relieved.

"First, I want you to know that the story you've just told me is very familiar," Beth said. "This often happens to new artists the first time they face the pressure of a big tour. Look at this."

She showed Elle a diagram of the larynx and the vocal cords and told her how the voice works and why certain things tax it more than others.

"Sleep is *big*. So are water and vocal rest when you are not singing. I have seen so many singers blow out their voices by doing interviews before the show. Talking really takes a toll on your voice. You have to protect your ability to do the show. The interviews can wait."

Elle soaked in her words like a sponge.

"Great singing is a combination of energy and relaxation," Beth continued. "Your body should be relaxed but engaged in using your energy and breath to sing."

Beth took Elle through several scales, starting low and working her way up.

She showed her where the healthy placement was in her voice. "Placement is where you hear your voice resonate," Beth said. "If you sing the word *sing* and hold out the *ng* sound, you should feel it resonate right in your nose."

It sounded strange, but Elle tried it. She touched the bridge of her nose and felt it buzz! Maybe it wasn't just voodoo and yoga and steroid shots. Maybe there was a science to singing after all. Maybe there was hope.

"If you are singing in a healthy placement," Beth said, "then your voice should not get tired from singing. It should actually get stronger. The problem comes when we sing beyond our comfort range too much and we don't take care of our bodies. Then the voice experiences fatigue. Think of your voice as a muscle. Like an athlete, you have to use your muscle properly. Take care of it, or you will damage it."

Beth took her through more scales and asked Elle what song gave her the greatest challenge. "'Breakdown.' It has a big vocal climb in the bridge. It freaks me out now when I try to go for it."

"Okay, let's work on it, but I want you to sing it in your head voice instead of your chest voice."

"What do you mean?" Elle asked.

Beth demonstrated. When she sang, the tone was pure and sharp. "This is all in my head voice. And this is my chest voice." This time the notes came out broad and large and much more mellow.

"And this is a mix of head and chest." When she sang, it was just that. There was still a warmth and bigness to the sound, but it was in total control.

At the end of the session, Elle felt that she'd learned more about her voice from Beth in ninety minutes than she had learned in her entire life.

* * *

The day of the show she woke early, stretched, ate a healthy breakfast and spent the morning being quiet. After a light lunch, she began doing the vocal warm-ups Beth had custom-made for her.

But her mind kept going back to what had happened the day before when she ate too much pizza. There was a word that was nagging her.

Bulimia.

A girl in Elle's high school had died of complications from bulimia.

Elle took a deep breath. She knew she had to get a handle on this. Maybe she even needed to tell someone, but who? Not her dad, that was for sure. Her mom would have understood. She felt so ashamed. What if word got out? That was all she needed. Another social media scandal.

She closed her eyes and tried to focus on her vocal warm-ups. Soundcheck was in an hour. She couldn't wait for this night to be over.

Sixteen

The media blitz before the show was completely insane, as was the meet and greet. This was when all the industry people and some contest winners got to meet the artists and have their pictures taken with them before the show.

Elle had taken Beth's advice and declined all interviews except for a brief one with Marsha's friend Deborah Evans Price from *Billboard* magazine.

They talked for a few minutes about Memphis and then about the show in Los Angeles. Elle knew that Deborah would write about her with compassion and respect, so she told her the whole story. The only thing she didn't mention was the pizza.

She smiled for pictures and shook hands with everyone from the mayor of Nashville to the star player for the Nashville Predators.

She saw lots of people from her label— Tommy, Grant, Jamie, her dad, Lesley. It was moments like this that the label people lived for.

She tried not to glare at Kara and Brian when she passed them in the line for meet and greet.

She was genuinely happy when she saw Marsha come in with a handsome guy in jeans and a cowboy hat. She hugged Marsha and was about to be introduced to her mysterious cowboy friend when Todd came and whisked her away to get ready for her set.

She noticed there had been no sign of the twins at the meet and greet. They were always there, front and center, soaking up all the attention and press. Posing for photo ops and kissing up to anyone they could.

Elle asked Todd where they were, and he made a kind of awkward face. "Yeah...about that. Some of the wives...after the LA show, they weren't digging the girls' trashy vibe. Said maybe we should consider some background singers who were a little more 'professional.'" He put the word in air quotes.

Elle had to suppress a smile. She had a very good idea which wife on the tour had the kind of power to make such a request.

"But you're in for a treat. The session singers who did the vocals on Johnny's latest album are gonna be filling in on the rest of the tour. Michael, Kimberly and Lisa. They are *amazing*. No egos, and they wear a lot more clothing."

Elle and Todd doubled over laughing and gave each other a high five. Her night was getting better already.

As they were walking back to her dressing room, she saw a very thin, frail-looking girl. She was standing in line to speak to Johnny, but when she saw Elle, she started waving. Elle asked Todd if she could say hi quickly. It wasn't good to ignore her fans.

"I am so excited to meet you, Elle," the girl said. "My name is Molly, and this is my mom, Samantha. We're here from Georgia. We won tickets to the show and a chance to meet you and Johnny James."

"That's so great," Elle said, wondering why no one had told her.

"Elle, I just want you to know that your music has really helped me. I-I have struggled for years with an eating disorder. Anorexia. I spent the last several months in and out of the hospital." Her mom stood quietly at Molly's side while she spoke, her love for her fragile daughter apparent on her face.

"I didn't know if I was ever gonna come out of it. But with some help I finally started to understand my disease. It's complicated, but part of it was my need to feel in control and to feel beautiful. When I saw your 'True Blue' video on YouTube, it connected with something deep inside me. I started to see things differently. So thank you, Elle. Thank you for being who you are."

Elle gave Molly a hug and thanked her and her mother. As she fought back the hot tears that threatened to run her mascara down her face, she thought about all the times she had binged and purged. And for what? To fit into a size 0 dress?

She went to her dressing room to freshen up, but she wasn't thinking about the show or the media. She was thinking about Molly. Something Elle had done had made a difference in someone's life. She knew why she needed to fight to record songs she believed in. She knew why she had to get her eating habits under control. She knew why she had to endure the stress of the road and surrender so much of her life to be an artist.

A word came to her. She was quite certain it was the word that would propel the rest of her career.

Purpose.

Seventeen

The knock came. It was time for the show, but there was something she had to do before the set started.

She walked straight up to Blaine, who was standing on the wing of the stage, ready to go on.

"Blaine, I have something to tell you."

"Ahh. Okay, sure. Show's about to start though."

"I know, but I can't let another minute go by without telling you how sorry I am for the whole episode in Memphis. For trying to use you to make Webb jealous."

"No sweat, Elle. I get it. Love makes you do crazy things."

"I'm sorry. Will you forgive me?"

"You bet. Now go out there and show 'em what you got, girl."

She smiled at Blaine as the lights dimmed and the band took their positions onstage.

When her cue came and she walked out onto the stage, it was if the trouble of the last month rolled off her shoulders.

It wasn't voodoo.

It was heart. It was soul.

It was what she had been born to do.

Sing. With purpose.

When the high notes came, she didn't worry. She just thought of Molly and all the other girls out there who were struggling to be true to themselves. She remembered everything Beth and Marsha and Karen had taught her.

Before she sang "Breakdown," she said, "There are times in your life when you lose yourself, lose what matters to you. You try to be something you're not. You find yourself falling apart. I just wanna say that it's never too late to turn around and find your way back home. I should know. Tonight I want to dedicate this song to a new friend. Molly, this song is for you."

No steroids, no technical tricks, just the songs and the gift she had taken for granted.

When she left the stage, everyone gave her high fives.

"Best show ever!"

"Elle, you killed it!"

Johnny James and Holly came back to congratulate her. Johnny said, "Elle, I know it took a lot to struggle through the last few weeks. We've all been there. Most of us have had to overcome some hard knocks. I'm sure proud that you got out there and won big."

"Thank you, Johnny," Elle said. "I really appreciate the opportunity you've given me, being on this tour. I've learned a lot, but I'm now more sure than ever that there's so much more to learn."

Then Johnny said something she knew she would carry with her forever. Something that separated people who tried to succeed from those who actually did.

"Elle, the minute we think we've got it all figured it out is the minute it's over. We are students of life. Every day."

Holly squeezed his arm and planted a kiss on his cheek. His smile could have lit up Greer Stadium.

What a great couple, Elle thought. They prove that you don't have to be a jerk to be successful. She hoped she would carry that lesson with her always.

She was grateful for how well the show had gone, but success was no longer the driving force in her life.

She cared about something much deeper. And she had never felt so glad. She went back to her dressing room. There was someone she needed to talk to.

She sent Webb a text. **Are you here?**

Yes. You were amazing. Btw.

:) Would you meet me later? I have something I want to tell you.

Yes. Text me when you're ready. I'll come find you.

When everyone had cleared out, Elle sent him another text. **I'm ready. Want to meet by the buses?**

When she got there, Webb suggested they go for a drive. She hopped in his truck, and they drove to a beautiful spot called Love Circle, up in the hills of Nashville. From there they could see all the lights of the city. It was romantic. Her heart beat a little faster. She had to remind herself what she wanted to say.

They found a place to park, and Webb said, "It's such a nice night. Want to take a walk?" They strolled along the circle that meandered around the top of the hill. Giant trees swayed over them. The city lights twinkled like the stars above them.

She was the first to break the silence. "I want to say I'm sorry. For how I've treated you. You have been the best friend I have ever had, and I have treated you like dirt these last few days."

"Elle, I—"

"No, let me finish. I've been so messed up. Worrying about what everyone thought of me. Worrying about pleasing my dad, pleasing Johnny James, pleasing the label. In the end, I was losing myself, forgetting what really mattered to me. The girl, Molly, that I dedicated the song to—she reminded me of why I am here and why I've been given the chance to have this career. A chance to make a difference."

Webb had stopped walking and was facing her now. Looking into her eyes like he couldn't see anything else in the world.

"There are some things I still need to deal with, to work through," Elle continued. "But I just wanted you to know how much you mean to me."

He took her hands in his, and they stood less than an arm's length apart.

Something like magic filled the air between them. Then he leaned down and kissed her. A kiss as tender as one of his most beautiful love songs. She melted into his arms as if it were the most natural thing in the world.

Eighteen

Early the next morning, Elle got an email from Tommy, asking her to come to a meeting later that day with Grant, Jamie, Steven and Bernie. *Elle, if you could be here at two o'clock this afternoon, we are going to be hosting two special guests in the meeting.*

That was all the note said.

Elle and Webb had been out till late, walking and talking and basking in the glow of their blossoming romance.

She shook herself awake, wondering what the meeting could be about. She didn't want anything to ruin the wonderful moment she was having in her life.

* * *

Later that day, Steve, Grant, Tommy, Bernie and Elle sat around the conference table with a glowing Marsha Chapman. She was accompanied by the tall cowboy she had brought to the show the night before. Everyone except Elle seemed to know who he was.

Tommy made introductions. "I'm sure you all know Marsha, and I am guessing most of you know Wilfred Worthington. Marsha brought Wilfred to the show last night, and he had some thoughts to share regarding a song he heard."

Elle's eyes almost popped out of her heard. There had been something familiar about him, but she couldn't place it until she heard his name. Wilfred Worthington was one of the richest men in America. He came from humble beginnings, a cattle-ranching family in Texas. As Elle would later learn, he was Marsha's next-door neighbor and high-school sweetheart.

Wilfred's family had struck black gold in Texas back in the eighties. One of the biggest gushers on record. No matter how rich they got, the family always kept a keen eye on the needs of those less fortunate. They were also generous supporters of the arts.

Wilfred had followed Marsha's career as a songwriter very closely. A music lover himself, he had decided to try his hand at owning a few radio stations. Texas was known for country-and-western music. It was the music he had grown up on, and he applied the same work ethic he had brought to being a cattle rancher and oil tycoon to his radio stations.

Now, seven years later, he owned a syndicated network of radio stations, called KISS Country, that played the hottest country music. Wilfred had hired experts from Nashville and LA to run his stations, but he himself kept a close eye on what was going on. He was always delighted to see Marsha's name on a song in heavy rotation.

"Wilfred, I'll let you take it from here," Tommy said.

"Thank you so much, Tommy. Gentlemen, I understand you have decided against singling the song 'Breakdown.' I don't mean to get in your kitchen, boys, but I am of the mind that it's a decision that bears more consideration. 'Breakdown' is a special song, as was made evident by the overwhelming response the song received last night."

He continued, "You would have had to have been dead not to feel the electricity in the audience as she sang that song. Pretty as a bird. I took the liberty of getting some of Elle's fans to fill out a form asking which of Elle's songs was their favorite."

Wilfred reached down and retrieved a worn and beautiful leather duffle bag that sat at his feet. He unlatched it and poured hundreds of small square questionnaires onto the table. He picked out a few and began reading.

" *'Breakdown'! My new favorite song!...* 'Breakdown.' *Man, that girl can sing...*'Breakdown.' *It made me cry!* And it goes on and on. Eighty percent of the people who filled out a question-naire chose 'Breakdown.' By the way, more than half of those people said the song made them cry. And you know what we like to say in the music business. *They cry, they buy.*"

Elle's heart was beating out of her chest. She felt more than a little embarrassed about the kind things people had said. She reminded herself to stay grounded. This was about a lot more than being right. She guessed that was something she would have to keep reminding herself.

Mr. Worthington kept going.

"As you know, KISS Country represents hundreds of country-music stations across America. We would be delighted to put 'Breakdown' into rotation. I have a feeling the song will find a life of its own. Sometimes you just have to take a chance and follow your gut and throw the testing out the window, boys." His cowboy smile was as charming as it was challenging.

Grant was completely tongue-tied. Jamie was shaking his head over the enormity of the commitment Wilfred had just made.

Elle could see that her dad was fighting the urge not to take Mr. Worthington's advice, but Jamie met his eyes with a look that could have burned a hole through glass. Bernie was practically drooling. His comb-over was drenched in sweat.

Her dad sat quietly for a bit and then rose and did what any smart businessman would do in that situation.

He extended his hand to Wilfred Worthington.

Elle could not believe the words when they came out of her dad's mouth. "Mr. Worthington. As you have said it, so it shall be. 'Breakdown' is the new single."

Elle couldn't hold back the emotion. Tears of relief and happiness and gratitude flooded her eyes.

Spontaneous applause broke out in the room. Everyone knew something big had just happened. Elle leaped from her chair and thanked Mr. Worthington for taking a chance on her. He saw her tears and gave her a very sweet, fatherly Texas hug, the kind that only men from Texas with big hats can give.

Then she turned to Marsha and gave her the biggest, tightest sister hug she could muster. She thanked her for everything she had done—and risked—for her.

"You guys belong together," she whispered in Marsha's ear.

Marsha blushed. "Thanks, darlin'," she said with a wink. "It's a long story. One I'll tell you sometime."

Elle's heart felt so full, she thought it would burst with joy. There was one person she could not wait to share it with.

After the meeting broke up, Elle walked out into the sunshine and texted Webb.

Where are you?

At the boat.

Meet me at Frothy Monkey for a latte.

Is everything ok?

Everything is more than ok. See you there in 20?

Wild horses couldn't keep me away.

* * *

They sat at a small table in the California-style coffee shop known for its healthy food and excellent coffee. Elle had ordered a green tea. It was time to start being responsible about her health.

She stared across at Webb. The late-day sun cast a golden glow around them as she told Webb about the meeting.

He was completely enthralled by her story. Every now and then he took her hand in his and squeezed it gently. He beamed at her. He was as happy for her as if it had happened to him. Happier even.

The air was sweet with the emotion flowing between them. It was something Elle had honestly never expected. She had always heard that some of the best relationships started off as friendships. She tried not to get too far ahead of herself. She just wanted to enjoy the moment. Being here with him, and enjoying the feeling of being happy.

Happy for the sense of purpose she felt as she moved forward into whatever this next phase of her life held. Happy for the good news from the meeting that day.

But what surprised her most was something she hadn't expected in the drama of the last few months.

A crazy little thing called love.